More **D**

First series

The Dark Fire of Doom	978-184167-417-9
Destiny in the Dark	978-184167-422-3
The Dark Never Hides	978-184167-419-3
The Face in the Dark Mirror	978-184167-411-7
Fear in the Dark	978-184167-412-4
Escape from the Dark	978-184167-416-2
Danger in the Dark	978-184167-415-5
The Dark Dreams of Hell	978-184167-418-6
The Dark Side of Magic	978-184167-414-8
The Dark Glass	978-184167-421-6
The Dark Waters of Time	978-184167-413-1
The Shadow in the Dark	978-184167-420-9

Second series

The Dark Candle	978-184167-603-6
The Dark Machine	978-184167-601-2
The Dark Words	978-184167-602-9
Dying for the Dark	978-184167-604-3
Killer in the Dark	978-184167-605-0
The Day is Dark	978-184167-606-7
The Dark River	978-184167-745-3
The Bridge of Dark Tears	978-184167-746-0
The Past is Dark	978-184167-747-7
Playing the Dark Game	978-184167-748-4
The Dark Music	978-184167-749-1
The Dark Garden	978-184167-750-7

Dark Man

Fear in the Dark
by Peter Lancett
illustrated by Jan Pedroietta

Published by Ransom Publishing Ltd.
Radley House, 8 St. Cross Road, Winchester, Hampshire
SO23 9HX, UK
www.ransom.co.uk

ISBN 978 184167 412 4

First published in 2005
Reprinted 2007, 2011

Dark Man

Fear
in the Dark

by Peter Lancett

illustrated by Jan Pedroietta

Chapter One:
The Rod of Iron

The Old Man comes to see the Dark Man.

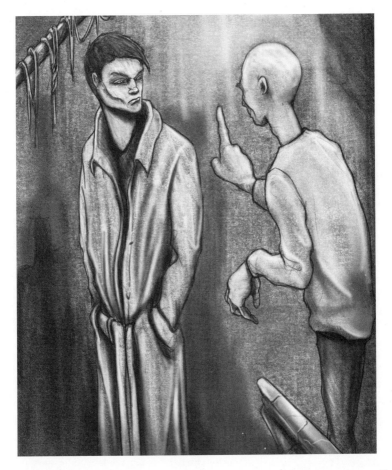

"They saw a Shadow Master in the city," the Old Man says.

The Shadow Masters are evil.

"What does he seek?" the Dark Man asks.

"The Rod of Iron," the Old Man says.

"The Rod of Iron can control the future," the Dark Man says.

"So you must find it first," the Old Man says, as he turns to go.

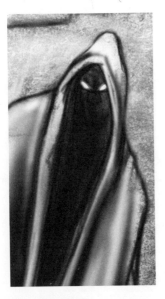

Chapter Two:
The Girl

Now the Dark Man sits in a coffee shop.

The Old Man said that a girl would help him.

How will he find this girl?

A girl sits at his table.

The Dark Man looks up from his coffee.

He did not see her come into the coffee shop.

She looks like an angel.

"I was looking for you," the girl says.

"So now you have found me," the Dark Man says.

The girl stands up.

"Shall we go?" she asks. "We do not have much time."

Chapter Three:
Faces in the Shadows

The girl takes the Dark Man to a bad part of the city.

The streets are full of broken glass and rubbish.

It is almost dark.

As they walk, the girl hangs back.

"What is it?" The Dark Man asks.

"I see faces in the shadows."

The Dark Man looks but cannot see them.

"The Shadow Master has sent things to stop us," the girl says.

Chapter Four:
Horror in the Dark

The Dark Man and the girl step into a hallway.

There is no light.

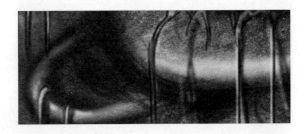

"The Rod of Iron is at the end of this hallway," the girl says.

They hear soft voices behind them.

The girl stops.

"I am afraid," she says. "It is too dark."

She begins to cry.

"Get the Rod of Iron," the Dark Man says. "I will stay here and protect you."

The girl moves forward.

The Dark Man can no longer see her.

He feels a push but stands firm.

He fights things he cannot see, but they
do not pass.

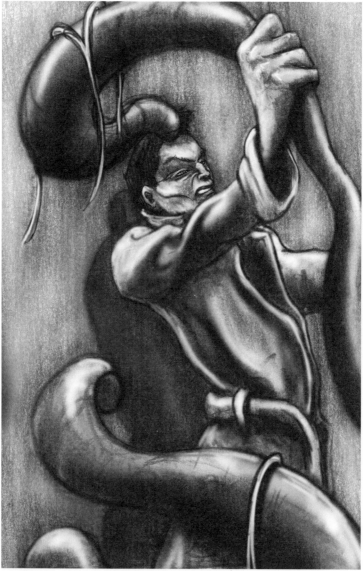

There is a scream that fills the hallway.

Then it is silent.

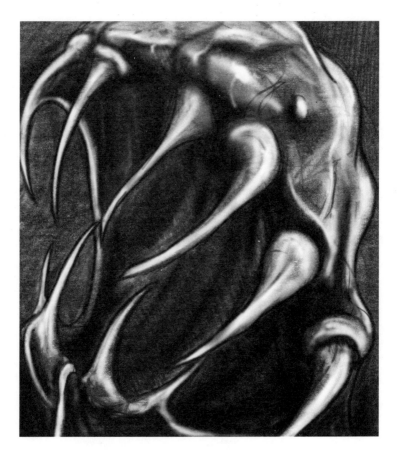

He calls to the girl but gets no reply and he cannot find her.

He steps out into the street.

Does the girl have the Rod of Iron?

He can only hope that she does.

The author

photograph: Rachel Ottewill

Peter Lancett used to work in the
movies. Then he worked in the city.
Now he writes horror stories for a living.
"It beats having a proper job," he says.